Suffering Substitutes!

Michael Coleman

Illustrated by Nick Abadzis

ORCHARD BOOKS

ORCHARD BOOKS
96 Leonard Street, London EC2A 4XD
Orchard Books Australia
14 Mars Road, Lane Cove, NSW 2066
First published in Great Britain in 2000
First paperback edition 2001
Text © Michael Coleman, 2000
Illustrations © Nick Abadzis, 2000
Cover photograph © Action Plus
The rights of Michael Coleman to be identified as the author
and Nick Abadzis as the illustrator of this work
have been asserted by them in accordance with the
Copyright, Designs and Patents Act, 1988.
A CIP catalogue record for this book is available
from the British Library.
ISBN 1 86039 937 1 (hbk)
ISBN 1 86039 938 X (pbk)
1 3 5 7 9 10 8 6 4 2 (hbk)
1 3 5 7 9 10 8 6 4 2 (pbk)
Printed in Great Britain

Contents

ANGELS F.C.

Coach

Left Full
Back

Midfield
(Centre)

Striker

Right Full
Back

Centre
Back

Goalkeeper

Kirsten
Browne

Barry 'Bazza'
Watts

Daisy
Higgins

Colin 'Colly'
Flower

Tarlock
Bhasin

Lennie
Gould
(captain)

Trev the
Rev

Substitute

Midfield
(Centre)

Centre
Back

Substitute

Midfield
(Right)

Striker

Midfield
(Left)

Mick
Ryall

Jonjo
Rix

Lulu
Squibb

Jeremy
Emery

Rhoda
O'Neill

Lionel
Murgatroyd

Ricky
King

1

Muscle Man...

"Coo-ee! Lion-el!!"

Lionel Murgatroyd's head turned slowly, but beneath his white gymnast's vest his heart was racing like an Olympic sprinter with his shorts on fire.

Nikki Sharpe, the most gorgeous girl in the gymnastics club, was heading his way!

"V– Vello, Hikki!" stammered Lionel.

"Pardon?"

Lionel struggled to get his tongue under control. "I mean, hello Veggie. No! I don't mean that! I mean Nikki!

That's it. Hello, Nikki!"

"Hello, Lionel," purred Lionel's dream girl.

She was holding a clipboard and carrying a pen between her slim fingers. Thrusting both into Lionel's trembling hands she asked, "Will you be the first person to sponsor me, Lionel? Per-leaase?"

Lionel's stomach did a backwards somersault. Sign her sponsorship form? He'd walk across a beam strewn with banana skins if she asked him to! Taking the pen, Lionel signed his name with a flourish. Only then did he wonder exactly what he'd signed. He looked at the printed section at the top of the form.

WALKING THE TIGHTROPE

I will be walking a tightrope
to raise money for the
Dudmanton Charity Fayre!
Please sponsor me for
as much as you can afford.

Lionel gulped. How much could he afford? Was Nikki Sharpe as good at tightrope-walking as she was at making his knees turn to jelly?

"How – er, how far do you think you'll get?"

"Oh, no more than four or five metres. I'm no good at it, really. You'd be much better. I've seen you on the beam. You're wonderful."

"Vanks merry thatch," gurgled Lionel. "I mean, thanks very much."

"You're so steady," cooed Nikki. She

bent down and gave Lionel's knees a little squeeze. "I wish my legs were as strong as yours...Muscle Man!"

Muscle Man! Lionel quickly put himself down for twenty-five pence a metre before he fainted with delight.

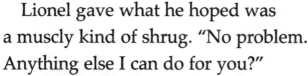

"Ooooh, thank you, Lionel!"

Lionel gave what he hoped was a muscly kind of shrug. "No problem. Anything else I can do for you?"

"Well..." Nikki Sharpe's eyelids fluttered. "A little birdie tells me you play football for Angels FC. You couldn't get the whole team to sponsor me, could you?"

"Sure! Leave it with me! I'll get them all signed up." *Even if I have to pay the money myself!* thought Lionel.

Nikki Sharpe sighed. "I love football! And I bet you're really good at it, aren't you, Lionel? Just like gymnastics."

Lionel bit his tongue. Much as he'd like to say it, he *wasn't* good at football. Gymnastics was his best sport. He could trot along the narrow beam as if it was a wide street. But play football?

Football was different. Lionel loved the game, loved everything about being part of the Angels FC squad – but a good footballer he wasn't. He couldn't run very fast, he couldn't tackle very hard and, worst of all, when Lionel kicked a ball it always shot off in the strangest directions.

That was what he should tell Nikki Sharpe. But, as he gazed into her deep blue eyes, he just couldn't bring himself to admit it.

Instead he said, "I'm...er...not *bad* at football..." *Which is true,* thought Lionel. *Sometimes I'm not bad. Sometimes I'm terrible.*

But Nikki Sharpe clearly wasn't convinced. "I think you're being a modest Muscle Man," she cooed. "I think you're really the best player in the Angels team. I bet you're near enough out on your own."

"Ah. Now that *is* near enough true," said Lionel.

It was, too. While the rest of the squad were playing on the pitch, he would be standing on the touchline along with Ricky King, the other Angels substitute. If that wasn't being near enough out on his own, he didn't know what was!

"Admit it, Lionel. You're their top player, aren't you?"

"Well," cried Lionel, truthfully again, "I've never been substituted!"

"A star footballer!" sighed Nikki Sharpe. "And a superstar Muscle Man for getting your less talented team-mates to sign my form!"

She took Lionel's quivering hand in hers. "You will come to the Fayre on Saturday and watch me walk the tightrope, won't you Lionel? Per-leaase!"

Lionel nodded furiously. "White rope talk at the hair on fatter day? Yes! Yes!"

Lionel couldn't wait until the next training session to get Nikki's form signed. Instead he took it with him on Sunday evening to the St Jude's Youth Club. All the Angels team were members.

"Ricky!" he called, seeing Ricky King the moment he stepped through the door. "Just the man to sponsor a tightrope walk."

"Sure, Li," said Ricky, signing the form at once. "Say, how long have you been a tightrope walker?"

Lionel looked down at the form. Nikki had forgotten to put her name at the top. He was about to say as much when he thought better of it. He would get the form signed a lot quicker if he didn't have to explain that he was doing it for a girl whose tinkling voice gave him goosepimples on his goosepimples.

"How long have I been a tightrope walker?" he said. "Er...not long."

Off he went around the room. He'd just managed to get the final signature when Trev, the Angels coach, bustled in.

"Attention, everybody!" he cried. "I've got some news about next Saturday's match."

Jeremy Emery frowned. "I didn't think we had one, Trev."

"We didn't," said Trev. "But we have now. I've just had a call inviting Angels FC to take part in a special friendly match against Royals FC."

The players exchanged excited glances. They'd heard that Royals FC were a good team, but had never met them before.

"It may be a friendly, but they're taking it seriously. I'm told they even had a spy at last week's match."

Lionel winced. The previous week, with Angels 4–0 ahead, he'd been sent on for the last ten minutes. By the time the final whistle blew they'd been pulled back to 4–3 and were hanging on by the skin of their teeth!

"Now I know it's short notice," Trev went on, "so is everybody available?"

Lionel looked round the room. For once he was pleased to see the nodding heads. It meant he wouldn't be needed...

"How about you, Lionel?" asked Trev. "I might need to call on you."

"Er..." began Lionel, wanting for once to say that he couldn't play – but definitely *not* wanting to say why! "I'm not sure, Trev. I kind of, er...promised to go to the Dudmanton Charity Fayre."

Trev grinned. "Then you *are* available, Lionel. That's where we're playing. The challenge match is one of the main attractions!"

At the Dudmanton Charity Fayre? The same Fayre that Nikki Sharpe would be at?

As the news sank in, Lionel's heart sank with it. A football-mad Nikki Sharpe would be bound to watch the match. And when she realised that one of the teams was Angels FC, she'd be bound to look for him. And when she saw that far from

17

being their star player, he was only their substitute...

It was too awful to think about. She'd either laugh at him or else tell everybody what he'd said so that *they* laughed at him. One way or the other he'd be made to suffer. He'd be a suffering substitute!

No, decided Lionel. Somehow he had to get himself into the starting line-up.

The question was – how?

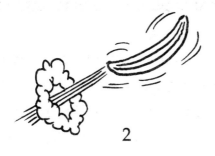

2

...Or Banana Man?

The obvious way to get picked was to turn in
a brilliant performance at training. If he did
that, Trev might put him straight in the team
for Saturday's match against Royals FC.

So it was a determined Lionel who
handed Nikki Sharpe her completed
sponsorship form at the gym club on
Monday evening...

"Thank you, Lionel!" she cooed. "You're
my little twinkling star!"

...And an even more determined Lionel
who turned up for training on Tuesday.

After their warm-up exercises and skills sessions, he elbowed his way between Colly Flower and Jonjo Rix to kick off for the Angels' usual practice match.

"Hang on, Lionel," said Colly. "I'm striker, not you. You usually play...er, *where* do you usually play?"

"Everywhere," said Lionel. "That's half the problem. I need to find my best position. I think it might be striker."

Too kind to tell Lionel that he'd be surprised if he could strike a match, let alone a football, Colly trotted back into midfield. More than that, when he won the ball from Rhoda O'Neill a few minutes later, he slid a perfect pass through to where Lionel was loitering, slap-bang in the centre of the penalty area. It was a golden chance for him to score.

"Aim for the bottom corner, Lionel!" Colly shouted encouragingly.

Lionel looked up at the goal, looked down at the ball, looked up at the goal again, picked his spot – and shot.

Wwwwwhhhhhhhhhhhhheeeeeeeeeeeeeeeeee!

The shot whizzed off his boot like a rocket – but, sadly, a rocket without a rudder. Heading straight for just a fraction of second, it then began to curve away from the goal...and away...and away...until, with a clatter, it smacked the corner flag out of the ground!

"I think Colly meant the corner of the goal, Lionel," shouted Jonjo, trying not to laugh. "Not the corner of the pitch."

Lionel sighed. Maybe striker wasn't the position for him after all. Maybe midfield was the place for him to be, spraying brilliant passes in all directions.

"OK, change over," he told Colly. "I'll play centre midfield, you be striker. And get ready for some special passes!"

Lionel's chance came as Daisy Higgins won a tackle and swept the ball to him. He saw at once that, up ahead, Colly was in bags of space.

"Get ready, Colly!" yelled Lionel, lashing the ball forward. "Here it comes!"

But, once again, almost as soon as it started, the ball began to curve wildly to the right...and curve...and

curve...until this time it knocked the centre-line flag out of the ground!

"Not quite a defence-splitting pass, Lionel," called Daisy. "More of a flag-splitting pass!"

Lionel scuttled up to her. "Maybe I'm really a defender. How about doing a swap?"

Daisy agreed, and back went Lionel into the heart of defence. Easy, he decided. With everybody except goalkeeper Kirsten Browne in front of him, even his worst pass would have to go near somebody!

He was wrong. Lionel had forgotten that defenders have to tackle.

The next time the ball came near him was when Lennie Gould, playing on the other side, swept through the middle only to be stopped by a last-ditch tackle from Jeremy Emery.

"Kick it into touch!" called Jeremy, as the ball bobbled free.

"Mine!" yelled Lionel.

Racing across he tried to hammer the ball away – only to see, yet again, the ball curve off to the right as if it was a rocket-powered banana and begin shooting towards his own goal! Only a wonderful save from Kirsten Browne stopped it from going into the net.

Lionel sank to his knees in despair. Out on the touchline, Trev was jotting something down in his notebook and Lionel had a good idea what it was: *Do NOT pick Lionel Murgatroyd, even if it means Angels take the field with only ten players!*

⚽   ⚽   ⚽

And so it was a stunned Lionel who was pulled to one side by Trev after training was over and told, "Lionel, you're in the team for Saturday."

Lionel's mouth fell open. "Wha– wha– what did you say?"

"I said you're in the team for Saturday," repeated Trev. "Mick Ryall will be substitute." Trev shook his head as he walked away, muttering mysteriously, "Sending me a petition. I hope they know what they're doing."

Petition? wondered Lionel. What was Trev on about? Lionel was too ecstatic to care. *He was in the team!*

Lionel did a handspring. He did a somersault. He did a handspringy kind of somersault with a treble twist and perfect landing. He was in the team, and Nikki Sharpe would see him play like...

Oh, no, realised Lionel. Nikki Sharpe would see him play like he usually played – hopelessly! Completely and utterly hopelessly!

And *that* would be even more humiliating than having her find out he was only a suffering substitute instead of a superstar.

Now he didn't want to be in the team after all!

3

It's Not Fayre!

A gloomy Lionel, sports bag over his shoulder, drifted through the gates of the Dudmanton Charity Fayre at 2 p.m. on Saturday afternoon. Hard as it had been, he'd come to a decision. He was going to tell Nikki Sharpe the truth about how useless he really was at football.

Off he went to search for her, hardly noticing the crowds as he pushed through them – and certainly not noticing Trev slip out from behind a tree and start to follow him.

Lionel had just reached some sort of football sideshow when he saw Nikki hurrying his way.

"Coo-ee! Lionel! I hear Angels FC are playing at the Fayre today! Oh, I can't wait to see my Muscle Man star in action!"

It was just the opening Lionel needed. "Er…look, Nikki. You've what it gong… I mean, you've got it wrong."

"Got what wrong?"

"About me being the Angels' star player." Lionel took a deep breath – then blurted out the truth. "I'm not a star. I'm hopeless, in fact. Useless. Totally, totally, useless."

He finished with a sigh then, shame-faced, looked down at the ground. *There, he'd said it.* But what would Nikki Sharpe say to him in return? Lionel was ready for a screech of anger, or a howl of rage. But not the silvery giggle he heard.

"Oh, Lionel you can't fool me. Useless, indeed! You're just being modest, I know you are!"

Modest? Modest? Suddenly it sank in. *She didn't believe him!*

"But I *am* useless! I can't play football for toffee!"

How could he convince her? A sudden shout from the nearby football sideshow came to his rescue.

"Roll up, roll up! Flatten the goalie and win a prize!"

The sideshow consisted of a goal – and a wooden goalkeeper on a stand. The idea was to hammer a penalty straight and true so as to knock the goalie over. What's more, Mick Ryall was about to try his luck. Perfect!

"Mick! Let me have a go first, eh?"

"Definitely," grinned Mick, standing to one side. "This I've got to see!"

Lionel turned to a bemused Nikki Sharpe. "This will prove it to you. A chimpanzee with a broken toe could do this better than me. I'm so useless I'll miss that goalie by a mile!"

No, thought Lionel as he got ready to take his shot. *I'll make it even more convincing. I'll use my left foot. Then I'll miss by two miles!*

He stepped back. He ran in. He hit the ball. Off it flew, perfectly straight…and stayed straight! Without swerving by as much as a centimetre it smacked against the wooden goalie and rebounded like a cannonball – straight into Mick Ryall as he stood watching!

"Ohhhh," groaned Mick, collapsing in a heap.

As Trev appeared – from nowhere, it seemed to Lionel – to administer first aid, Nikki Sharpe seemed almost as stunned as Mick.

"Fan...er...tastic, Lionel! You...you *are* a star. Didn't I say so!"

Trev gave Nikki a quizzical look, before turning back to the groaning Mick. "No game for you today, Mick," he said. "Not even as a substitute."

Now what do I do? thought the suffering Lionel. Nikki Sharpe didn't believe him and Mick Ryall couldn't take his usual place in the team even if he'd wanted to. *How could he get out of the game?*

"I hope Ricky's here," Trev was saying. "We won't have a substitute if he's not."

Ricky! That was it. He would find Ricky and ask him to play instead. Then Lionel could go back to being substitute. If Nikki Sharpe asked why, he'd pretend to have injured himself tripping over a candyfloss or something.

"Are you coming to watch me tightrope walk then?" asked Nikki.

"Yeah, but...er... I've just got to do something first. I'll catch you up!"

Leaving a frowning Nikki Sharpe to go her own way, Lionel hurried off in search of Ricky King.

He found him fifteen minutes later – or, rather, Ricky found him.

"Li! Here, man! You're just the dude I need!"

Ricky was standing near another football sideshow called *Three-Legged Shoot-Out*.

"Be my partner, Li!" urged Ricky, before Lionel could say a word. "We've got to tie our legs together, y'know, three-legged style, then dribble a ball down and bang it into the net. Quickest time today wins the prize."

Lionel looked at him in amazement. "And you want *me* to be your partner? Miskicker Murgatroyd?"

"Sure, I do. You're a gymnast, man! Running in a straight line and keeping your balance is easy for you."

"Kicking the ball straight isn't."

Ricky waved away the objection. "I'll do that bit. You just run."

Seconds later he'd handed over his money and a man had strapped Lionel's right leg to Ricky's left. A ball was put in front of them – and they were off!

"Go for it, Li!" yelled Ricky as they spurted across the ground in perfect co-ordination, "we've got this sewn up!"

On they went, up to the penalty area, the ball still at Ricky's right foot.

"Hit it!" yelled Lionel.

"I can't!" screamed Ricky. The ball, hitting a bump in the ground, had bobbled away from him and in front of Lionel. "You hit it!"

Lionel didn't have time to think. The ball was in front of him. But his right leg was attached to Ricky's left. There was only one thing to do. For the second time that day he smacked in a shot with his left foot... and, for the second time that day, he hit as straight, as true, as rocket-like a shot as any player had ever hit before. In the blink of an eyelid the ball

screamed into the net, catapulted back out
again – and promptly clobbered Ricky!

Yet again, Trev was miraculously near
by. He dashed over, helped revive the
crumpled Ricky, but then confirmed
Lionel's worst fears.

"Ricky's out of action too. He's going to
have a bump on his head the size of an egg.
A dinosaur's egg."

"You mean..." began Lionel.

Trev nodded. "Yes, we're down to eleven fit players. You'd have been playing anyway." He looked hard at Lionel. "That petition wasn't needed."

Petition? thought a confused Lionel. *What was Trev on about?*

He couldn't hang around to find out. He'd run out of people to take his place in the team. There was only one thing left to do.

Lionel hurried off towards the Dudmanton Charity Fayre Tightrope Challenge.

And so, a short distance behind him, did Trev.

4

Don't Look Down!

Lionel's mind was made up. He didn't want to be in the team. Not only would he make a fool of himself in front of Nikki Sharpe, but, even worse, he would let the rest of the side down. In fact, the more he thought about it the more he decided that the Angels would be better off playing with only ten players.

And ten players was what they would be left with if he got himself injured! After all, he'd accidentally injured both Mick and Ricky. Injuring himself on purpose should be easy! And what better way than to do it than in front of Nikki Sharpe's very own eyes?

"Coo-ee! Lionel!" trilled the girl herself, appearing at his elbow the moment he reached the Tightrope Challenge. "I couldn't wait for you to arrive, so I've just had my go. Guess what happened!"

But Lionel wasn't interested in guessing. He was more interested in the quivering tightrope. Stretched between two high posts about ten metres apart, it was perfect! Take a nose-dive off that and he would definitely do himself a mischief!

Only then did he notice, to his dismay, that beneath the rope layers of soft, spongy matting had been put down for people to fall on to without hurting themselves. It wasn't fair! How could he hope to give himself a decent injury with those mats there?

At his elbow Nikki Sharpe was still talking, only less patiently. "Don't guess, then. I'm going to tell you anyway. Look!" She pointed at a small flag stuck in the ground about six metres from the start of the tightrope walk. "My marker! I'm in the lead!"

"Great!" cried Lionel.

"Oh, enthusiasm at last."

But Lionel hadn't been enthusing over her performance. He'd just seen the solution to his problem. He needn't worry about the mats. All he had to do was tightrope walk as far as that nice pointy flag, then jump on to it. A hole in his foot would be sure to keep him out of the game!

Quickly, he handed over his money and climbed to the starting platform.

"What are you doing?" cried Nikki Sharpe anxiously. "Get down. You've got a football match to play in."

"I don't want to play in it," Lionel shouted back. "They'll do better without me!" And with that, he stepped out onto the rope.

It was just like being on the beam at gymnastics, only a bit thinner and more wobbly. But, holding his arms out wide, Lionel got himself nicely balanced – then off he went.

One metre. Three metres. Five metres. Six metres!

He could see the pointed marker flag sticking up invitingly, all ready for him to jump on to...

"Keep going! You're the best so far!"

Lionel could have cried. The man in charge, who was following him along beneath the rope, had just plucked the flag out of the ground. It wasn't there to jump on to any more!

There was only one thing to do. The landing mats ended at the finishing pole. If he walked the whole length of the tightrope he could launch himself off the end and on to the lovely patch of rock-hard ground beyond the mats. That should get him a broken ankle at least!

On he went. Eight metres. Ten metres. He was at the end of the rope! Time to jump!

"Stop!" screamed a girl's voice near by.

"Yaaaaahhhhhh!" yelled Lionel as he fell – only to land on the soft, comfortable mat Nikki Sharpe had managed to shove beneath him just in time!

Lionel was furious. But then so was Nikki. "You broke my record," she said furiously. "Well, you broke my fall!" Lionel retorted.

"Of course I did! You could have hurt yourself and missed the match!"

"But I wanted to miss the match! I keep telling you. *I'm no good at football!*"

Nikki Sharpe's eyes glittered wickedly. "Tell me something I don't know," she said.

"What?"

"I know what you're like at football!" snarled Nikki Sharpe. "I spied on your last game, the one where you came on for the final ten minutes. That's when I came up with my petition plan to get you into the Angels team for today."

45

Lionel looked at her, mystified. "Petition plan? What petition plan? And why would you want me in the team anyway?"

"Because she plays for Royals FC Lionel," said a familiar voice near by.

Nikki Sharpe looked up at Trev and laughed nastily. "Too right! And with Miskicker Murgatroyd here playing for your lot, we're definitely going to win!"

5

Lionel Lines Up

Stunned, Lionel watched Nikki hurry away laughing.

"I don't understand," he said sadly.

"I think this will explain it," said Trev, holding out a sheet of paper for him to look at. "It dropped through my letter box before training on Tuesday."

The sheet was covered in the signatures of the

47

Angels players. At the top it read.

> We, the undersigned, reckon that
> Lionel Murgatroyd should be in the team
> for the match against Royals F.C.
>
> *Lionel Murgatroyd*

So this was the mysterious petition
Trev had been on about, realised Lionel.
The petition in Nikki Sharpe's plan!

"I thought it was genuine at first," said
Trev. "That's why I put you in the team."

Lionel sighed. "But it was a forgery.
What she needed was all the Angels
signatures. She just pretended to like me
so that I'd collect them all for her on her
petition form."

"But Nikki made one big mistake. She
forgot that you wouldn't have put your
own name down first on a petition asking
me to pick *you* for the team," said Trev.

"When I looked more closely at it yesterday and saw your name right there at the top, I realised something fishy was going on. That's why I've been following you around all afternoon – to see if I could solve the mystery."

"And now you have," said Lionel, glumly. He looked down at his feet. "She was right to want me in the team though, wasn't she? I *am* rubbish. She's right when she says they'll beat us with me playing."

Trev put his arm round Lionel's shoulders. "I don't think she is, Lionel. Not from what I've seen of you this afternoon. You've got talents I never knew you had."

"I have?" gasped Lionel. "What talents? What are they? Tell me, tell me, tell me!!"

Trev simply smiled. "I'd prefer you to discover them for yourself, Lionel. But here's a clue. You're playing on the left wing!

Left wing? Lionel was still thinking as the match got under way. *What sort of a clue was that?*

Lionel hadn't the faintest idea what to do on the left wing. So when Rhoda O'Neill played the ball out to him after five minutes, he turned inside and tried to hit a through pass for Colly Flower. But, as ever, the ball squirted off his right foot, bending like a banana, straight to a Royals player who was only stopped by a crunching tackle from Lennie Gould.

Not long after exactly the same thing happened again. An attempted pass straight across the half-way line curled in the air and only just reached Kirsten in the Angels goal before the Royals striker could get to it.

"Keep it up, Lionel," Nikki Sharpe taunted, running past. "You're doing everything right – for us!"

Lionel was going to shout something back when he stopped in his tracks. What had she said? *You're doing everything right?*

Right? Suddenly the memories of that afternoon came flooding back. His *left-footed* penalty that had rebounded and brained Mick Ryall. The *left-footed* shot that had rebounded and flattened Ricky King. Trev must have seen them both. Could that be why he'd put him out on the left wing?

He was still thinking about this as Tarlock Bhasin, receiving the ball from Kirsten, played it on down the line.

"Lionel!" screamed Jonjo Rix, running into a gap in the Royals defence, "Hit it!"

Lionel did just that. Stopping the ball with his right foot, he turned and struck it with his left. Ping!

Without swerving by a single centimetre, Lionel's pass put Jonjo in the clear. All the Angels striker had to do was race on and bang the ball past the Royals goalkeeper to put Angels 1-0 ahead!

"Luck!" sneered Nikki Sharpe. "You won't do that again."

But Lionel did do it again. Again and again. Across the field, down the wing, at all sorts of angles, Lionel's left-footed passes couldn't have gone straighter if they'd been world-champion homing pigeons.

Nikki was getting narked. As Lionel slid yet another left-footed pass just out of her reach midway through the second half she snapped, "Right! You *definitely* won't do that again."

Lionel laughed. "Don't you mean, 'Left! I definitely won't...' *Aaaaggghh!*"

With a scything tackle, Nikki Sharpe had charged in and cracked him hard on the left ankle.

While the referee gave her a stern lecture for the ferocious foul, Trev raced on and sloshed cold water over Lionel's ankle. By the time he'd finished Lionel was able to run again but the moment he tried to kick the ball with his left foot a fierce pain shot up his leg.

"Said you won't do that again, didn't I?" hissed Nikki Sharpe.

"Do you want to come off, Lionel?" called Trev.

Lionel refused. But soon he was wondering if he'd made a bad mistake. Unable to use his left foot, his game was back to its normal hopeless self.

An attempted pass inside to Lulu Squibb banana-ed away over Jeremy Emery's head and allowed the Royals striker to run through and hit the ball past Kirsten. 1–1!

More right-footed passes went astray, the ball curving round like a boomerang every time he hit it with his right foot. It was awful. Every time Lionel got the ball the Angels ended up going backwards!

Soon, the whole team didn't dare venture forwards. Encouraged by this, Royals swept on to the attack, leaving a miserable Lionel standing out on the left wing.

"Lionel!" It was Trev, moving towards him and pointing down at the white touchline. "That line is a gymnastics beam. Got it?"

He didn't get it, but Lionel nodded anyway. "For the last ten minutes of the match I want you to run up and down on it. Don't move off it at all."

Lionel nodded again, glumly. He knew what Trev was doing. With his one talent no longer working he was keeping him out of the action.

Or was he? Because Trev then added, "And listen for my instructions!"

So for the next few minutes Lionel trundled up and down the touchline as carefully as if there actually was metre drop on both sides. Meanwhile the Royals mounted attack after attack.

Then, with a superb interception, Daisy Higgins broke clear for the Angels. A swift pass forward found Lulu Squibb. She turned past her marker and clipped an angled ball on to Jonjo Rix...only for Jonjo to be heavily tackled. The ball squirted free, bobbling towards the touchline ahead of Lionel.

"Go, Lionel!" cried Trev. "But stay on the line!"

Lionel spurted forward, reaching the ball just as it was about to go out of play. Then, obeying Trev's instructions to the letter, he began to dribble the ball along the touchline.

Now Trev was running beside him. "Keep going Lionel, keep going..."

Lionel ran on. He was almost level with the penalty area. What was Trev thinking of? Was he getting him to dribble the ball down to the corner flag to waste time?

It seemed he was. For, still running beside him, the Angels coach was shouting, "Now when I say, hit it as hard as you can straight at the corner flag! Wait for it, wait for it..."

Lionel dribbled and waited, dribbled and waited – until suddenly Trev screamed, "Now!"

In a blur of movement, Lionel did what he'd been told. He looked up, took aim at the corner flag, and hammered the ball right-footed with all his might.

Off scorched the ball, bang on target. Until, as ever, it began to curve and curve...away from the corner...across the penalty area...over the head of the Royals goalkeeper... and into the net!

2–1 to Angels! And a goal to Lionel!

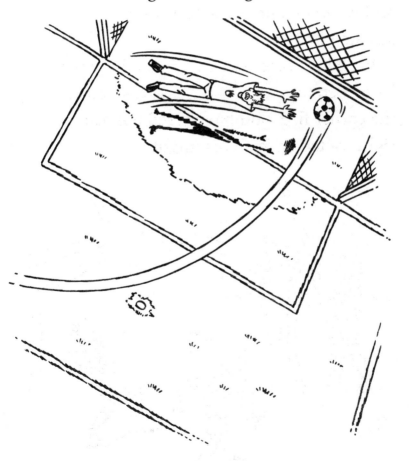

"Well done, super-sub," grinned Trev as the whistle went for full time. "Three prizes at the Fayre and a winning goal! Like I said, Lionel, you've got talents!"

"A great left foot," nodded Jeremy Emery enthusiastically.

"And an amazing banana shot from the left wing," laughed Lulu Squibb. "How on earth did you work that one out, Trev?"

The coach smiled. "Simple, really. Whenever Lionel aimed at the goal he'd hit the corner flag – so I thought if I encouraged him to aim at the corner flag he'd hit the goal!"

"And he did! Two talents found in one day," said Jonjo Rix.

Bazza Watts pointed, "But one girl lost, by the look of it."

A scowling Nikki Sharpe had collared Lionel and was obviously telling him what she thought of him. Finally she turned round and flounced away, her nose in the air.

"She called me a rotten cheat," said Lionel. "Said I'd only pretended to be hopeless and that anybody who could do banana shots like that had to be half Brazilian at least!"

"So, no more Nikki," said Bazza Watts. "Are you suffering from a broken heart?"

Lionel's face split into a wide grin. "Nah. She was starting to drive me round the bend!"